SWEET DETAILS:
MOUNTAIN MERMAIDS:

SAPPHIRE LAKE

PA VACHON

ME, MYSELF, & I PUBLISHING

About this book:

Shield Maiden Hedda Karoline Lofbald was cursed along with the rest of her clan when their Chieftains son scorned a powerful witch.

Now many years later Hedda meets Travis when she is on land during one of her monthly jaunts under the full moon...will the curse be broken, or will her watery prison remain her forever home.

ACKNOWLEDGMENTS

Without the amazing trip we as authors took in April of 2018 this series would never have happened. There are only three of the five 'original' authors who published this round and I have to thank two of them. Moxie you are still one of the nicest, truest people I have ever met. PJ, you amaze me ever day with your talent, your generous soul and your dedication. To Grace, thank you so much for coming into this small world with us. I loved your book. To Desiree, for your first foray into PNR you hit it out of the park lady.

To Meester PJ, thank you so much for doing this cover again for me! I love it. You are so talented.

I can't put out a book with out thanking you, my readers. You guys keep me going like nothing else. I am so appreciative of you as readers, friends and my reader family. I don't think I would be publishing today without your support!

And as always to my number one supporter, my husband. You are still my greatest ally and the one who shelters me when the going gets tough. I love you more today than I did yesterday. I will love you even more tomorrow. You are my heart and my soul. Forever...

PROLOGUE

The red flames licked at the wood, and as the orange and yellow danced in the darkness she couldn't help but compare it to the burn of green and blue that had sealed the fate of dozens of people, including herself.

Tamsin had once loved who she was. She had been bound to the earth for as long as she could remember being aware of herself. Her land had flourished; a perfect circle of life. That was until the strangers came. She watched as they prayed to Gods she didn't know. She kept her distance and saw they respected the land, so she didn't begrudge them the food they took to eat or the animals they chose to sacrifice. They seemed like decent humans. Some of them were even desirable to look upon, for mortals, that is.

In particular, she had watched a man who was handsome and brave. Although younger, he seemed to be a leader. There was one above him, a father figure that constantly put him in front to lead the group.

She shouldn't have cared. His life was short compared

to her own, as a powerful witch she was eternal and she had never considered any needs that would be physical. But this man made her think of things that she shouldn't have even bothered with. They called him Bjorn. She came to him one day while he was sitting on the edge of the lake where his clan stopped for a time. It was one of her favorite lakes with stretches of crystal blue water and under the surface were blue stones that she loved to collect.

When she appeared, he was frightened. Vikings feared the unknown and the occult. She'd clothed herself in what she thought were clothes that looked like his, but she couldn't hide the magical glow that always encircled her. When she finally started to speak he had started to back into the lake, his feet dipping into the waters.

She told him she wouldn't hurt him, that she wanted only to help. He stayed and listened, and in the days that followed, Tamsin met him again, and again, by the edge of the lake, and she showed him the blue stones she liked to gather. He seemed very excited when she showed him. Tamsin wanted to please him and showed him where they could find them at the bottom of the lake.

Day after day their strongest swimmers would swim down and come up with the stones. One day, one of them never came up. The clan mourned his loss but didn't stop their diving.

Tamsin found that she was falling a little more in love with Bjorn every day. One night she stayed with him, their bodies joining in what could only be called divine, if there was such a thing. Bjorn's people called her a witch. She'd been called many things and this name didn't bother her any more than others.

One day, she came down early hoping to surprise him. She'd visited another lake nearby and brought him some stones that were as clear as air. She hoped he would like them. What she found was him mating with a woman from his clan. They were rutting on the shoreline, their naked bodies flashing in the sunlight.

Her shock turned to anger, then into something that didn't even have a name. Tamsin's soul splintered and she'd never felt such pain. She couldn't figure out how to make it go away. All she could think of was to make Bjorn feel like she did. She first approached his father and told him of her betrayal by the hands of his son. The man laughed at her and told her it was their way. Everyone was free to choose who to love and who they shared their bodies with.

Tamsin couldn't understand their cruelty, and his laughter echoed in her mind and fueled her rage. Her next actions were ones she would have to live with forever.

She told Bjorn that she understood their ways. She lied so convincingly. Bjorn told her they had more stones than they could carry and would be heading home... without her.

Tamsin gathered them together and promised she would bless their voyage home and would be waiting for them when they returned. To ensure their prosperity they need only build a replica of their vessel that had brought them to her land. She would bless the vessel and them, ensuring an easy journey and a swift return.

They worked on the boat together, decorating the sides with paintings that told stories of selkies and mermaids. A wooden serpent with an open mouth and flaming tongue was mounted on the prow of the ship and looked dangerous and strong much like the explorers themselves.

To complete the ritual, she encouraged them to board the boat and row to the middle of the lake. As they waited for her blessing, she saw Bjorn staring back at her, but his eyes reflected none of the love she once was so certain she had seen.

> *"A love so true, the earth rejoiced.*
> *A betrayal so cruel, the stars cried.*
> *Those that chose to ignore my pain,*
> *Will forever be bound to the bounty they*
> *Tried to steal. My heart is shut to their*
> *Cries of pain. Your souls will twist in*
> *The mud below just as the fish dig for food.*
> *You'll suffer as I have under each full moon.*
> *Until such time that you find your true love."*

As she spoke her words, the ship burst into flames. The fire licked at those on board, the blue flames not burning but covering them, their skin changing color to match the fire. Their legs melted together in a magical swirl and they collapsed upon the deck, their tails slapping desperately. As the ship sank the final echoes of those on board calling for help, begging for mercy, rang in the air.

From above she saw a brilliant flash of light that seemed to have come from the heavens above. She could hear the sounds of those above her, the old gods that came before. They cast down a blessing over her curse. Those below the water would be protected. The bow of the ship touched the water and the serpent came to life, its long body moving to encircle the boat.

The old gods promised they would sleep and only awake when they could find their true loves. Their magic was strong, much stronger than hers. There was no breaking her curse and no matter how the old gods tried to help, the explorers from the north would never forget what price they had paid to cross Tamsin.

Once the ship sunk under the water, Tamsin made her way to the surrounding lakes. She found more of the explorers, ones that had traveled with Bjorn and his clan.

They all were taking from the lakes without giving back. She repeated her curse on all those that had sought to steal the heart of the lakes.

Someday, many moons from now, Tamsin knew she might one day regret what she had done. Until that day, she would make sure that the people of the lake knew unending days with no love in their hearts.

CHAPTER 1

Hedda Karolina Lofbald spent her days swimming in the waters of Sapphire Lake. She had been swimming these waters for more years than she cared to remember. Only touching land for three days a month during the full moon. This was the time that was used to search for that special someone who could break her curse. The curse of the witch Tamsin. Who'd made the mistake of falling for Bjorn, the Chieftains son. You can't choose who you love. You can only choose to give your heart and hope that it's not returned to you broken and bleeding.

Hedda didn't blame Tamsin for her feelings of rage that lead to the curse imprisoning the clan in Sapphire Lake, she blamed Bjorn and his fickle heart. Taking and taking. Never giving. Hedda had made the mistake of falling for Bjorn as a young woman. He had broken her heart as well. So, no she couldn't be mad at Tamsin. She could only swim in the lake and hope that the next time she gave her heart, it was given to someone worthy of her love and devotion.

Pulling her thoughts from her musings, Hedda swan for the labradorite fields beneath the waves.

At the fields Hedda scanned the lake bed for the main mineral that the people of the lake traded with the towns-people to barter for goods that she needed during her forays on land. Those three days were getting harder and harder. Looking for her mate was becoming a pipe dream that she wasn't sure would every see the light of day.

CHAPTER 2

Travis Schmidt stood with his employers of the last five years, Tom and Julie Jones. He'd been employed at Sweet Treats Bakery since graduating Pastry Arts classes at Seattle's Culinary Academy. A grueling program that he at times thought he might not survive. Saying goodbye to his strongest supporters was proving difficult. Mr. and Mrs. Jones had helped him achieve the title of Seattle's Best Baker of 2018. They had nurtured a shy, somewhat nerdy twenty-two-year-old into a confident, albeit still nerdy twenty-seven-year-old. He hated that the older couple were retiring and headed to the Florida Keys, but he understood their need for warmer weather. Seattle's rainfall and chilly mornings made it hard for the elderly couple to get into the bakery every morning by three am. For the last year, it had been his job to prep the bakery for their 7 AM opening. He would arrive every day just before 3o'clock, he would turn on lights as he entered and then begin his actual day by sanitizing the kitchen area and set the large industrial oven to pre-heat then go about preparing the dough needed to make bread, buns and all sorts of other baked good. Once he finished those tasks, he would move on to mixing ingredients that were required for all of the products they sold throughout the day such as whole grains and cheeses for scones, fruit filling for Danishes and the like. By the time he turned the open sign over to allow customers to enter, he would have been working in the bakery for four hours. Within the first hour of the doors being opened the shop located on California Avenue would fill with customers for their early morning coffee and pastries, others would arrive to purchase fresh baked bread to have with their dinners later in the day. Just around noon time, Travis would give the kitchen another thorough cleaning and prep for the next day would begin. With just him and Mr. and Mrs. Jones working the bakery by the end of the day when they closed at 5 pm the kitchen had been cleaned again and the register and the paperwork would be completed so that he could go home for the day.

He loved the flexibility of working in the bakery. He would take a long break near the middle of the day, just before the second cleaning of the kitchen.

Throughout the day, he could be seen bustling between the back-kitchen area and the display cases at the front adding fresh baked goods as they were whisked away by their regulars. His was a good job, he hated to be unemployed, but he had a plan. A plan that included a bakery of his own. Not in the Seattle Metro area, he couldn't afford to live and own a business in the area. He had started to look online for bakeries that might be up for sale. He was looking in all sorts of places in the US and Canada. Travis's dads' side of the family was originally from the Montreal area and he had kept his dual citizenship current. It paid to have parents from two different countries.

CHAPTER 3

Travis stood in line at the airline counter to get his boarding pass. He had decided he needed to visit the town of Aurora Falls to check out the bakery he was interested in purchasing.

The Jones' had offered to let Travis purchase the place he'd worked for the last five years. Unfortunately, Seattle was too expensive for Travis to even consider the offer. So, he'd gone to bakeriesforsale.com and discovered that the small town of Aurora Falls had a small mom and pop bakery for sale. He'd finally found the perfect sounding bakery that was for sale in a small tourist town on the shores of Sapphire Lake in the newfoundland area of Canada. Looking down at his phone for what was probably the seven hundredth time, Travis read the ad again. "Small town bakery for sale. Price Negotiable, willing to train right person to take over also comes with a small cottage."

Travis was overjoyed when he came across the ad a little over two weeks before. After letting the Jones's know he couldn't afford to stay in Seattle. He scoured the internet and lucked upon this little gem. He couldn't wait to get to Aurora Falls so he could see the bakery in person. The photos on the sale site were few and a little grainy, so the bakery interior was still a mystery. He didn't care how much work it needed, he somehow knew that he was supposed to be in Aurora Falls. That it would be the perfect place for him to get started on his own life. Getting through the security line, Travis headed for his gate. Just another two hours and he would be on his way.

TRAVIS STOOD OUTSIDE of Sapphire Lake Bakery looking at the "For Sale" sign in the window. He could picture the barren front window filled with sweet treats. Cupcakes, cakes, scones and cookies all made with love. He was ready to go back to Seattle and close up that chapter of his life and come back for a new beginning.

CHAPTER 4

Having arrived in Sapphire Lake from Seattle, Travis was just starting to get settled. He had loved working at the bakery but it had closed last week. Travis looked around the town square and took a deep breath. The clean air clearing his lungs. He was already feeling lighter, happier. The town of Aurora Falls was situated in the valley between mountains and the shores of Sapphire Lake. The bakery located on the main road across from the shoreline. The picturesque tourist town seemed to call to him. He felt like he had to be there, today. He packed up his belongings, sold what wouldn't fit in his car and drove for days. Arriving in town the night before, he'd rented a room at the Lakeview Spa and Retreat temporarily while he looked for a small house to purchase.

Staring into the window, pulling himself from the last few days of memories, he looked out over the lake.

The early morning mist coming off the lake was ethereal. Almost haunting in its beauty. Admiring the view for a few more moments, Travis smiled to himself and started for the door.

Opening the door, the bell attached to the inner handle giving a cheery ring as he entered the bakery. After walking to the large display case, he stopped and looked at the man behind the counter.

"Hi, I was wondering if the owner was in?" Travis asked the older gentleman behind the display case filled with sweets.

"Well, yes. You're in luck. I own this fine establishment." He answered with a smile, "Name's Bill, what can I do for you?"

"I saw your for-sale sign in the window, and was wondering what you're asking for the business?" Travis asked with interest.

"Well, the wife and I are wanting to retire and spend our days sitting on the deck looking out over the lake." Bill answered, "I have the place listed for $20,000."

"Really? Twenty grand? That's it?" Travis said in confusion, "Is business slow?"

"Slow? Nope, we get a steady business. We're the only bakery in town. The grocery store down the street doesn't even have one inside." Bill said, "The place is only twenty thousand dollars because we want to help out the next person who buys it. Pay it forward so to speak."

"I have so many questions." Travis said, "How soon are you looking to sell?"

"The sooner the better," Bill replied, "Retirement couldn't come soon enough."

"Let me think on it. I am a pastry chef/baker and would love to own my own place." Travis explained, "I just need to do some research first. Thank you for the information. Can I come back tomorrow and talk with you about what I decide?"

"Of course, that would be great." Bill replied.

Travis thanked Bill and left the bakery, heading

towards the lakeshore as he contemplated the fact that his dream was finally within his reach. Standing, looking out at the placid surface of the lake Travis thought about the cost of the bakery. The price was right. The location was amazing, right on the lake but far enough back that if there was a flood the bakery wouldn't be damaged by rising waters. Lost in thought, Travis missed seeing the woman watching from the lake, her eyes just barely above the surface.

Turning from the lake, he wandered to the center of town. Traveling aimlessly, not really with any destination in mind. Thinking more about the bakery and what Bill had said. This seemed like the perfect town to settle in and start living his dreams.

Stopping to look around Travis saw that he was outside of a small bar. Looking up he could see the name of the bar on the sign above the door.

The Saucy Wench est. 1965.

Looking at the front door of the bar, he grasped the ornate handle which was shaped like a mermaid on the prow of a ship and opened the door. Even though it was still very early in the morning the bar was open for breakfast. Felling like he could eat Travis entered the bar, looking around he felt as if he had been transported back in time. The bar top was one long mahogany counter with the lower walls of the bar painted a light teal color. Mismatched barstools set at the counter, but they worked in the space. They looked like they'd always been there, even with the different colored seat cushions and scarred up legs showing that for a small-town bar, many patrons frequented it to enjoy a beer and bar fare.

Standing behind the bar wiping out a glass was the

tallest guy Travis had ever seen. Striding towards the bar, Travis stopped at the first stool he came to and sat down.

The bartender set the glass he'd been polishing down "You must be new in town. I've not seen you in before" the bartender stated in a friendly voice, "I'm Orion, welcome to my bar."

"Hi, I'm Travis, yes I did just arrive in town." He answered, "I'm looking for a change. Sapphire Lake sounded like an ideal place to relocate to."

"It is one of the best places in my opinion." Orion said, "What can I get ya?"

"I'd love a big breakfast. Eggs, bacon and some biscuits with gravy would be great." Travis answered.

"You're in luck, that's what we're serving today," the bartender laughingly replied, "How do you want your eggs?"

"Over easy and could I get a cup of coffee?" Travis asked.

"Sure, no problem. Give me a minute to put your order in and I'll get you that coffee."

"Thanks, it's appreciated." Travis replied as he watched Orion walk toward the order window that was set into the wall at the end of the bar top.

After several minutes, Orion returned with Travis's coffee asking,

"Did you need cream or sugar with that?"

"Nope, Black is good. Thanks." Travis replied.

"You seem pretty young to retire, what kind of work do you do Travis?" Orion asked.

"I'm a baker. Or pastry chef, depending on your point of view." Travis answered. "I used to work for a Seattle bakery, but the owners decided to close down and retire to the Florida Keys. I couldn't really afford the rent and the cost of the bakery. Then I was looking online and saw that the Sapphire Lake Bakery was for sale and I thought, this, this I could afford. This is where I'm meant to be."

"Order up!" Was called from the pass-through window. Orion left to get Travis's breakfast. Returning he set it on the bar top along with two bottles one of ketchup and one of hot sauce.

"Can I get you anything else, before I leave you to your meal?" Orion asked.

"No, thanks. This looks great. I can't wait to dig in." Travis answered, "Hey, before you go back to work, can I ask you a question?"

"Yeah, of course." Orion replied, "What's up?"

"So, I was wondering what else there is to do in town?" Travis asked, "Is there any entertainment I should know about?"

"Well, there is my bar obviously. There's also some water activities in the summer if you swim or boat." Orion said, pausing momentarily to think. "We also have a festival in the spring, as well as other outdoorsy activities like hiking, biking and the like."

Laughing, Travis said, "So, just a few things then..."

"Yep, a few." Orion said. "I'll let you eat. Holler if you need anything else."

"Will do, Thanks." Travis said as he put the first bite of fluffy biscuits and thick country gravy into his mouth. "Mmmm, that's good. I need the recipe for these biscuits. They are amazing."

Orion headed back to the kitchen area to start prepping the bar for the day. While in the dish area, he let his line cook, Sam, know that his food was appreciated.

Back in the main bar area, Travis was daydreaming of his ideal shop. Glass display cases across the front of the kitchen bisecting the space, with a register in the midst of the displays. An upgraded espresso machine to create top of line frothy hot coffee drinks. A Hobart, to mix the dough for all the pastries that he would sell to please the townspeople. Chocolate éclairs, Danishes, so many varieties of pie and so many other sugary treats. A sugar coma was almost always a wonderful thing.

Travis finished up his breakfast and flagged down Orion for another refill on his coffee. Sipping the hot, rich brew he continued to daydream about opening a place of his own. Deciding he needed to get his dream off the ground he headed for the Lakeview Spa and Retreat. The proprietor, Dawn was an interesting combination of new age hippie and take-charge business woman. Laying a twenty-dollar bill on the bar top, Travis stood up and headed for the door and his future in Aurora Falls.

Walking down the main street Travis spied several businesses that seemed to be doing a brisk business. Mermaids and Moonstones, a small gift shop that catered to the tourist, Legends and Tails bookstore, and a small diner that was further down on the lake, making it difficult to see the name of the establishment. Travis couldn't wait to be a part of the business community and lay down new roots.

Arriving at the Spa, he headed down the long driveway and to his assigned cottage, the pastel pink of the outer walls a foreground for the crystal-clear blue lake beyond. If he didn't know the retreat was full, he'd think that Dawn was yanking his chain and having a laugh at his expense. He was so not a pastel pink kinda guy. Opening his cottage door, he went inside and opened his laptop. Logging into his online banking information, he saw that his loan application was done being processed and he had a new message waiting in his inbox. Clicking on the icon in the upper right corner he opened the newest message.

Inside it read:

Congratulations! We here at Treeline Credit Union have approved your loan request in the amount of Forty-five thousand dollars. We will need you to e-sign a few documents before depositing the funds into your account. Please complete the attached documents at your earliest convenience. Thank you and have a wonderful day.

Sincerely

Patty Bright

Loan Processing Manager

Treeline Credit Union

Travis let out a whoop of excitement, clicking on the link he began accepting the documents, signing each one as he read them. When he reached the final document, the last paragraph stated that he would have access to his funds within 48 hours. Clicking the last e-sign button at the bottom of the last page with gusto, Travis let out a final whoop of triumph. His dream was finally becoming a reality.

CHAPTER 5

Hedda was getting antsy, the moon would rise tomorrow, and she would once again be able to travel around Aurora Falls. She could visit the Saucy Wench, Orion was always a good distraction from the prison that she had been encased in for centuries. Hedda knew that she had plenty of time to find her one true love, but she was starting to think that her Fated Mate would never show up in town. Last year, her clansman Tait had found his one true love. Phi was a dynamo of a woman who had broken the curse for Tait. They were now expecting a little one of their own any day. That was one place that Hedda definitely needed to stop once she was above water again. Tait and Phi had opened their home to her several times over the last few months. She needed to repay their kindness. Before the curse, whenever she was home, she loved to do metal work and make jewelry. She had the perfect stones to make Phi an amulet to wear. With that thought, Hedda headed down into the abyss of the lake. Swimming deeper and deeper, until she came upon her cave. Entering the cave, she veered to the left and the anti-chamber that had an open ceiling creating an air pocket and a two-foot shelf that extended from the walls where she could do her metalcraft on the side of her cave without getting completely out of the water.

Humming to herself, Hedda grabbed her jewelry supplies and got to work on a labradorite amulet for Phi. Taking the thin wire she'd purchased the last time she was in town, she swam to her labradorite stores and shifted through her favorites, picking one of the largest stones she swam a foot away and set all the items on the shelf on the side of the cave. Taking a moment to see the design in her mind, she began to wind the wire around the large multi-colored stone. Swirls of silver wire crisscrossed the stark colors of the labradorite. Once she had the wire wrapped as she wanted, she made a loop on one end to create the top of the pendant that would hang from a sturdy piece of leather that she would buy once she was in town. Placing the completed pendant in one of her waterproof boxes, she set it aside and left her cave to explore the lake bottom for more labradorite that she could use to trade for goods when she went to the surface.

As Hedda swam the lake bottom, she thought back to just before the clan was cursed. Several weeks before Bjorn had met Tamsin the witch, he had been following her around the village, by the third week of his attentions, she had finally said yes to him. A maiden still at the age of twenty, Bjorn had taken her virginity in a night of horror. No soft touches and kisses, it was all rough hands and forceful thrusts. Hedda was ever hopeful that her Fated Mate would be a gentler soul than Bjorn had been those two weeks she'd spent under his charming spell. Of course, that was normal behavior for the clan. Hedda had spent years and years eavesdropping on the young adults of Aurora Falls. To hear them tell it, sex could be a soft gentle breeze or a category four hurricane. Hedda was hoping for something in between.

Sifting through the silt on the lake bottom, Hedda came across a large chunk of rock that wasn't quite like what she usually discovered in the lake. She would have to take it to Gary, at the Aurora Falls Gem Emporium. Gary was always fair when he would trade with the Mer. If it was something of value, Hedda would be able to get more stores for the upcoming winter months.

Abandoning the search for other Labradorite she swam back to her cave to await the full moon that was just twenty-four hours away.

CHAPTER 6

Travis stood outside of the bakery, his nerves jangled from the amounts of coffee he'd already consumed over the last several hours while he drafted his offer for the business that he hoped to make his own. Watching Bill and his wife bustle back and forth from the open kitchen behind the glass of the front windows he could imagine himself in that space, every day, baking and visiting with the townspeople and tourists alike. Gaining the courage to open the door, he stepped into the fresh smell of baking bread and sighed happily.

"Well, hello stranger. Would you like an Aurora Falls Cinnamon roll?" Bill called from by the display case, smiling in welcome.

"Hi, Bill. I'd love one." Travis answered, "and maybe a minute of your time?"

"Sure, let me just let Lena know I'm taking a minute away from the front." Bill said. "Lena! Lena, I'm taking a minute love. Can you come out front?"

"I'm coming Bill," could be heard from the back of the kitchen, "There's no need to bellow for gosh sake."

Bill laughed, rolled his eyes then grabbed a cinnamon roll and walked around the display case to where Travis was sitting at one of the tables by the front display window. Bill placed the cinnamon roll on the table in front of Travis and then pulled out the second chair at the table. Sitting down he looked at Travis for a moment before saying,

"What can I do for you?"

"Well, Bill I'm hoping to convince you to sell the bakery to me." Travis said, "I know you and your wife want to retire and spend time together. I want to make a full price offer. Here is are the details."

Travis slid the sheaf of papers across the tabletop and watched Bill with apprehension. Waiting for him to take the papers and study them, Travis felt like time stood still as he worried that Bill would change his mind about selling.

Bill took a few moments, deep in thought and then picked the papers up and started to read.

Travis watched Bill's face as he perused the offer. His face gave nothing away. After several minutes Bill broke out in a huge smile and said,

"Well son, I think we might have a deal. Let me talk to the wife and I'll be right back."

Bill stood and walked to the kitchen area and began speaking to his wife. Travis couldn't hear the words that were being said but he could see Lena's face as she contemplated whatever it was Bill was saying. After several more moments, Lena smiled and shook her head vigorously in a yes motion. Travis tensed as Bill started back towards the table. Waiting for his answer.

"Well, you have a deal. How soon do you want the place?" Bill said gleefully.

"Really?" Travis asked, "Just like that? You don't need more time to think it over?"

"Travis, are you trying to talk me out of the sale?" Bill asked on a short laugh.

"NO! No, of course not." Travis replied, "I just didn't think it would happen in the space of a fifteen-minute conversation is all."

Bill watched Travis's face as the reality of the situation began to sink in. The smile that lit from within him was one of pure joy.

"Bill, I would love to start as soon as possible. I have some ideas on how to make the bakery my own." Travis said, "You won't mind if I change the inside and the signage, will you?"

"Of course not, once the place is yours you can do whatever you want." Bill replied, "Let's meet at the bank tomorrow and sign the rest of the paperwork to transfer ownership and get you started."

"Sounds good." Travis said, "Thank you both so much." Travis left the bakery with an enthusiastic wave towards the kitchen and a promise to see Bill tomorrow.

Walking along the downtown sidewalk towards the lake, Travis stopped and tried to catch his breath. He couldn't believe his dreams were coming true and in such a quick fashion. Starting to walk again, he detoured out to the lakeshore and stood unseeing across the smooth surface of the water. Travis didn't know it yet, but the lake held even more dreams than he could ever realize.

Travis would be having a celebratory drink later. He wondered if there was anything special going on at The Saucy Wench later today.

CHAPTER 7

Hedda watched as the sun began to sink from sight. The moon was already in the sky, shining down on the lake. She could feel the pull to leave her watery prison like a thin rope from the middle of her chest. Tugging her ever closer to the shoreline. She had to wait until the sun was completely down to leave her place in the water. As the last rays of the sun disappeared behind the mountains surrounding the valley, she slowly swam closer.

Reaching the shore, she left the water. As the cool wetness slid from her tail. A shimmer could be seen glowing slightly around her lower extremity. In a few moments where there once was a shimmery green, blue and gold hued scaled tail, were a pair of human legs. Slowly to get her land legs back after almost a month of swimming in the lake, she took a moment to breathe in the night air. Adjusting to being upright on her feet again.

Once she was settled and could walk a straight line, she headed for The Saucy Wench to see how Orion was doing. Arriving at the door, she grasped the handle and opened it wide. Walking inside she saw Orion filling a wine glass for a woman at the bar. Hedda walked up to the bar top and signaled the other bartender, Sean for a Mermaids Breath beer. The only thing she drank when she came onto land and visited with Orion at his bar.

Turning from the bar, Hedda scanned the mid-week crowd. The place wasn't packed, but there were several people sitting around the bar. At one table a man sat alone. Drinking a beer and smiling to himself. He was gorgeous. Strong jawline and smile lines around his mouth which would suggest that he was a happy guy. Dark blond hair that was cropped close to his head. She couldn't see his eyes from where she sat, but she wondered what color they were and if they lite up when he spoke. Hedda decided that maybe he could be her distraction from going back to the lake in three days. She wanted to find her Fated Mate, but she wasn't holding her breath. Picking up her beer, she crossed the room to the man's table.

"Is this seat taken?" Hedda asked

"Um, no. You can have the chair if you need it." He replied. "I'm not expecting anyone."

"I was actually wondering if I could sit with you." She said.

"Oh, ugh. Yes, please sit." The man said.

Hedda pulled out the chair and sat. Looking into the man's eyes, which were a sea green, she said,

"My name is Hedda. What's yours?"

"I'm Travis. Travis Schmidt." He replied, "Are you a long-time resident of Aurora Falls?"

"I am," Hedda replied, "A very long-time resident. Are you here on vacation?"

"No, actually I just put an offer on the bakery here in town." Travis said, grinning. "The offer was accepted and so I'm here having a drink to celebrate."

"That's great." Hedda said, "So, you bake? Or do you just run the business?"

"I'm the baker," Travis replied. "I can't wait to start making changes to the existing business."

Travis was animated as he spoke about the changes he was going to make.

"I plan on painting the walls a pale blue. I want to add newer, larger display cases at the front and then upgrade the kitchen equipment."

"That sounds lovely," Hedda said, "I can't wait to come in and try some of your baked goods. How soon do you think you'll be able to open?"

"I'm thinking a few weeks, four at most." Travis answered. "I'm looking forward to the work of getting the place to where I envision it."

"I'll bet, it sounds like you have a lot of big plans." Hedda replied, "I would love to help you celebrate."

Hedda lowered her lashes and peeked at Travis, hoping he'd see her invitation in her downturned gaze. Waiting for him to say something was torturous. She was about to tell him she'd see him sometime at his bakery, when he reached across the table and took her hand. Running his thumb across the back of her hand, he turned it over and continued to run his thumb across the sensitive flesh of her palm. He seemed fascinated with the spot just above her wrist. Looking closer in the dim light, he raised an eyebrow and asked,

"Where did you get this amazing tattoo? It looks like scales on a fish."

Hedda startled and pulled her hand back. Rubbing her mate mark, which did look like a watercolor tattoo she looked up into Travis's eyes and lost her train of thought. He was so amazing to look at and his gaze didn't seem to see anyone else in the room. Hedda couldn't believe that she'd found her mate. The one person who could see her *foflekk* or birthmark in English was the one person who could break her curse. The marking wasn't really a birthmark, it was placed there by their gods when they tried to counteract Tamsin's curse, along with the serpent that patrolled the lake. If Travis really could see her mark, then she would be able to be human again full-time. She would no longer have to swim the depths of Sapphire Lake and she would no longer be alone.

Travis watched as Hedda drew into herself. Confused as to why she would react that way to a question about a tattoo.

Pulling herself from her churning thoughts Hedda replied,

"It's not really a tattoo."

"It's not?" Travis said, "Then what is it?"

"Let me ask you a question first," Hedda said, "What does it look like to you?"

Travis looked at Hedda and then tried to formulate an answer for her.

"Well, its rough like scales. It's a beautiful combination of green and blue.' Travis stated, "Iridescent in appearance, almost like a watercolor tattoo."

Hedda contemplated what Travis had said. While technically he was right about the looks of her mark, he was wrong about it being a tattoo. It was really the mark of the gods as a way for the Mer to be able to tell when their Fated was near. It was the only way for them to break the curse and become fully human again. Hedda was a mass of emotions. Happy, confused, and apprehensive at the same time. The indecision must have shown on her face, because Travis took her hand again and gave it a small squeeze in support.

"I want to get to know you better, Travis." Hedda said

"I'd like that." Travis replied, smiling as he brought her palm up to his lips. Placing a small kiss there he squeezed her hand once more before placing their intertwined hands on the table between them.

Hedda took a sip of her Mermaids Breath and then smiled back at Travis. She could feel hope blooming and it was an amazing feeling.

"Would you like to take a walk?" Hedda asked once they'd finished their respective drinks.

"I'd like that," Travis answered as he stood from the table. Giving her hand a tug, he helped Hedda from her chair. Waving to Orion they both left the bar and headed towards the lake. The moon shone across the still waters, reflecting brightly.

CHAPTER 8

Once they reached the lake, Hedda and Travis strolled along the shore. Each step they took was bringing them closer together. It was if they'd known each other for a lot longer than just a few hours.

"When do you start working on the bakery?" Hedda asked.

"First thing after we sign the paperwork at the bank tomorrow." Travis answered. "I'm still in awe that my plans are coming to fruition."

"I'll bet," she replied. "Are Bill and Lena going to stick around while you get it ready to open under new ownership?"

"I know they plan on staying at least a few weeks," Travis said, "Bill wants to make sure I know what I'm doing before he leaves town for retirement."

"I don't blame him, they've owned the place for at least twenty-five years." Hedda said.

"You've known them that long?" Travis asked, "I bet you were a cute kid."

Hedda didn't want to lie to Travis, but she also wasn't ready to tell him about her life in Aurora Falls and the curse she'd lived under for hundreds of years. She might look like she was only in her late twenties, but curses were good for a girl's skin. She had been born in 975 BC after all.

"I was a handful that's for sure." Hedda answered.

"What do you do?" Travis asked, genuinely curious about Hedda's life.

"I mine for Labradorite, it's a pretty good way to make a living." Hedda answered, "I also make gemstone jewelry in my spare time. I have a piece that I need to deliver tomorrow actually."

"I'd love to see your work; do you live in town or out further?" Travis said.

"I'm around the lake over that way." Hedda said gesturing to the west side of the lake, "Do you see those cabins there on the opposite bank?"

Travis looked across the darkness to the other shore, seeing lighted windows a few hundred yards from the shoreline he said,

"Yes, I see them. Is that where you live?"

"Yep, my cabin is towards the back of that grouping." Hedda replied, "What about you? Where are you staying at?"

"When I got to town, I got a cabin at the Lakeview Spa and Resort. The pastel colors are a little girly, but the place is really peaceful." Travis said, "Although, I'm moving soon. Bill and Lena have a small cabin not too far from the bakery that comes with the purchase."

"That sounds nice." Hedda said. "I hate to end the night early, but I have several things to do tomorrow and not a lot of time to get them done."

"That's ok, I have to meet Bill pretty early myself." Travis agreed. "I'd like to see you again if that's ok."

"I'd like that." Hedda said.

"Let me walk you home." Travis said.

"Let's go." Hedda said.

Travis took Hedda's hand and they walked around the lake to the cabins that were lite in the distance.

Coming to the door of her cabin Hedda said,

"Thank you for walking me home."

"You're welcome, I'm going to kiss you now." Travis said, leaning in he tilted his head and covered Hedda's lips with his own in a soft kiss. Nothing more than a meeting of lips. It was the gentlest kiss Hedda had ever had.

Breaking contact, Hedda drew in a long, deep breath. Taking one hand she caressed Travis's cheek as he nuzzled her forehead. Leaving small kisses along her brow line. Hedda didn't want the night to end, but she knew that Travis had a lot to get ready for. Owning a business was hard work.

"Good night, Travis." Hedda said softly.

"Good night, Hedda." Travis replied, "I hope I see you tomorrow."

Travis watched as Hedda went into her cabin and closed the door. Waiting a moment to hear the lock turn, he then spun and headed back to the resort to get a good night's rest before his meeting with Bill.

CHAPTER 9

Travis woke at eight am. Stretching and yawning. He was ready for a cup of coffee and some breakfast. Travis couldn't wait to get into his own place again. It had only been a week since he'd arrived in town, but he was more than ready for his new life to begin. Rising from the bed he went into the restroom and turned on the shower. While he waited for the water to warm, he thought back to the previous evening when he'd met Hedda. She was beautiful. Long dark hair, bright blue eyes and legs that went on for days. She was every man's fantasy come to life. Stripping off his boxers he stepped into the spray of the shower still thinking of Hedda's curves. Within a few seconds his morning wood had returned from his erotic thoughts of Hedda. Taking himself in hand, he tightened his hold on his cock and stroked from base to tip. Seeing Hedda in his minds eye, his strokes hastened, on a groan his cock spurted his release against the tile wall. With the edge taken off, he could maybe get through his day without embarrassing himself.

After dressing for the day, he headed for the main building of the resort to have breakfast and coffee. Seeing Dawn at the front desk he stopped to say hello.

"Hey Dawn, how are you doing today?" Travis asked.

"I'm good Travis," Dawn answered, "How are you?"

"Good, I'm headed for some coffee and breakfast." Travis said, "Then I'm off to meet up with Bill to finish the paperwork on the bakery."

"That's so exciting," Dawn replied, "I'm so happy for you and the town. We get to keep our bakery."

Travis chuckled as he stepped through to the dining room. Grabbing a coffee cup and a plate he headed for the buffet. Filling his plate with eggs, bacon and toast, he next headed to the tall coffee urn and filled his cup. Going to a table near the windows that overlooked the lake he sat and added cream and sugar to his coffee. Sipping the hot brew slowly he inhaled the clean scent of the morning and the lingering smell of sage. Dawn was a friendly hostess, but she had some strange ideas. She was a cross between a hippie and a savvy business woman. A true paradox.

Finishing his breakfast, Travis left the resort and began the short walk to the bank. Arriving ten minutes later, he could see Bill already inside the bank speaking with one of the tellers.

Going through the glass front door, Travis called out,

"Hi, Bill. Hope I'm not late."

"Nope, you're right on time Travis." Bill answered back, "This is Jake. He's one of the assistant managers here at the bank."

"Hello, Travis." Jake said, "I hear that you're buying the bakery."

"Yep, I sure am." Travis replied. "It's nice to meet you Jake."

"Great, now that the pleasantries are out of the way let's

head to my office and get this deal signed off." Jake laughingly said, "Shall we?"

Jake led the way to his office. Bill and Travis following behind. Both men lost in thought. Each thinking of the turn their lives had made in just twenty-four short hours. Jake stopped behind his desk and waved a hand at the two wingback leather chairs that stood facing it.

"Please, sit." Jake said, taking a seat and opening a file folder that was sitting atop his barren executive desk.

Both men sat, watching as Jake went through the paperwork in the file. After several moments Jake looked up from the information in front of him and said,

"I see that all the documents are in order. Travis, will you be paying Bill in a cashier's check or cash?"

"I think a cash payment should be good." Travis said. "What do you think Bill?"

"That work for me and Lena." Bill answered.

"Ok, then I just need a few signatures on these pages here." Jake said, "Sign each place you see a red flag on the page and initial where the blue flags are please."

Travis and Bill took turns signing and initialing the contracts. Once they were both done signing, they shook hands with Jake and left the bank together. Walking down the sidewalk towards the bakery Travis and Bill kept up a running conversation.

"Do you think you'll need Lena and I for long?" Bill asked. "We'll stay for as long as you need us."

"I think a couple of weeks should do it, Bill." Travis replied.

"Good, that's good." Bill said, "Let me take you by the cabin before we go to the bakery."

Bill took a left at Main Street and headed towards Elm Avenue. Coming to Elm, he made a right and stopped in front of a small cabin that was painted a soft grey with white trim. It looked to be about 1200 square feet. The perfect size for Travis, who had left behind a 560 square foot apartment in Seattle. Going up the walk towards the front door, Bill pull a key ring from his pocket and unlocked the front door. Entering the cabin, the first room through the front door was a small living room on the right and a small office space to the left. Off to the right of the office was the eat in kitchen. Off the living room to the left you took a small hallway back to the two bedrooms and shared bathroom.

"It's perfect for my needs Bill." Travis said.

"I'm glad it will work for you." Bill replied, "Let's head on to the bakery, shall we?"

After touring the quaint space Travis and Bill headed back down Elm Avenue to Main Street where they then continued on to the bakery.

Entering the bakery Travis took a moment to stare at the interior space with a sense of pride. He was now the proud owner of his own bakery. He couldn't wait to see it once the remodel was done.

"Bill, Lena thank you for allowing me to buy your bakery." Travis began,

"It's your bakery now Travis," Lena said. "I hope you love it as much as we have over the years."

"I think I already do." Travis responded.

With a small laugh Lena turned to the kitchen and cleaned off the work table. The bakery was open and had been doing a brisk morning business. Now at just after ten am, it was starting to quiet down as it always did at that time of the day.

"Bill, can you give me some names of some contractors?" Travis asked as he sipped a cup of coffee. "I'd like to get some of the remodeling done this week. I think I'll need to close for a few days for the big stuff, like the new display counters and windows. But for the smaller things like new paint and signage, I should be able to stay open."

"Yeah, of course. Let me get my phone book." Bill answered as he headed to the office to get those numbers.

"Ah, here it is." Bill came back out holding a small leather-bound book. Turning to a middle page he recited the number for A1 contracting and repair.

"I'll call them in a few minutes." Travis said, "Are you sure you don't mind that I'm making some changes to the bakery?"

"Of course we don't." Bill said as Lena nodded her head in agreement. "You need to make it your own."

"Yes, you're right." Travis agreed. "I do need to make it mine."

Travis excused himself and stepped outside to watch the lake as he called the contracting company.

CHAPTER 10

Listening to the phone ring, he was staring blankly out towards the middle of the lake, hearing the machine pick up he left a quick message before hanging up the phone. Suddenly, someone stopped in front of him blocking his view.

"Well, good morning handsome." Hedda said leaning up to kiss Travis's cheek. "How are you? Did you get your paperwork taken care of like you wanted?"

Travis smiled down at Hedda and said, "As a matter of fact I did. Come in and say hi to Bill and Lena."

Travis gripped Hedda's fingers lightly, leading her into the bakery.

"Bill, Lena could you come out here please?" Travis called into the back.

"Sure, Travis." Bill called back. "Be right there."

Bill and Lena came out from the back and upon seeing Hedda they both stopped and stared at where Travis was holding her hand. Lena got a huge grin on her face. Bill looked a little more concerned, but that was just his nature.

"Well, Hedda dear, how are you?" Lena asked. "We haven't seen you in almost a month."

"I'm good Lena," Hedda answered, "I've just been busy."

Lena gave her head a shake. Having been a resident of Aurora Falls for all of her almost fifty-five years she knew about the legends of the lake. She'd heard all the stories. She also knew them to be true. Lena had known Hedda since she herself was five years old. Hedda hadn't aged more than a few years since then.

Lena's parents had meet one full moonlit night. Lena's mother had been cursed to live in the lake just like Hedda. Lena's mom had found her one to break the curse, Lena was born nine months later. When she was old enough, she chose to live on land full time. She'd met Bill and didn't want to go between the two worlds. Bill and Lena went on to have three children, before her parents had passed the children were spoiled by their doting grandparents. They were also told all of the secrets of the lake. To help protect the inhabitants and to keep the legends alive so that their little town didn't disappear like so many other small towns across the country.

Hedda watched Lena from her vantage point at the counter. She'd known little Lena for almost fifty years. Time seemed to pass so slowly in the lake. Then she'd come out during the full moon and the changes were staring her in the face. She could still remember like it was yesterday carrying Lena on her hip. She'd been there when Lena had married Bill at the young and tender age of just eighteen. When their children started to come along, Hedda had treated them like nieces and nephews.

She couldn't believe that little Lena was leaving their small lakeside community to retire. Hedda would miss them both.

"Lena, will you and Bill still visit after you move?" Hedda asked curiously.

"Yes, we will." Lena answered with a smile on her face, "This is our hometown, we could never abandon this place entirely. But we do want to be closer to the grandkids."

"I can understand that," Hedda said.

Travis watched the interaction between Hedda and Lena with interest. He saw a beautiful woman speaking kindly with a life long friend and he wanted to get to know that woman better.

"Hedda, would you like to take a walk with me?" Travis asked, "We can talk more about that amazing 'not' tattoo that you have."

Lena, overhearing Travis let out a small gasp. Hedda gave a small shake of her head, and then answered

"I'd love to take a walk. Where would you like to go?"

"How about down the street for some lunch?" Travis asked, "Maybe The Saucy Wench? I could go for a burger."

"Sounds good to me," Hedda answered, "I love Orion's cook, the food is awesome."

"It's agreed then, let's go." Travis said as he took Hedda's hand and left the Aurora Falls bakery.

"Are you excited still about the bakery?" Hedda asked as they walked the few blocks to The Saucy Wench.

"Excited, nervous and a little nauseous." Travis ruefully replied.

Hedda gave a small huff of laughter and shook her head.

"You're funny. You'll be ok." Hedda said.

They arrived at The Saucy Wench and headed inside. Taking a seat at a table near the bar they waited for the waitress to come and take their order.

"What looks good to you?" Travis asked, holding Hedda's hand and looking into her eyes.

"Hm, I think a double bacon cheeseburger and onion rings." Hedda answered, "Along with my favorite beer, Mermaids Breath."

"That sounds good," Travis said, "I think I'll have the same."

Just as he finished speaking their waitress arrived and took their order saying,

"I'll be right back with your drinks. Your food will be just a few minutes."

"Thank you, Lesa." Hedda said to the harried waitress as she hurried away from their table to take more orders. For being the middle of the day the bar was packed.

"So, how long before the bakery is remodeled?" Hedda asked Travis.

"Probably two weeks," He replied, "There isn't a lot that needs to be done. I'm just waiting on a call from the local contractor that Bill recommended."

"Was it A1 Contracting and Remodel?" Hedda asked.

"Yeah, how did you know?" Travis questioned curiously.

"It's the best in town." Hedda replied, "It's the only contractor that Bill uses, ever."

"That makes sense that you know who it is then." Travis said.

Lesa came back at to the table and placed their food in front of them. Travis and Hedda both started on their onion rings. Making quick work of the tasty, crispy o's.

"These are so good," Hedda said, "I miss eating them."

"Do you go out of town often?" Travis asked.

"Not that often," she replied, "but I am just back from an almost month-long trip. Actually, I have to leave again the day after tomorrow."

"You do?" Travis asked, "Work related?"

"Sorta, yea." Hedda replied. "But, I'll be back in town in

about a month. Maybe we can get together for dinner or a drink when I get back."

"Maybe," Travis agreed, "Are you going to finish telling me about your 'not' tattoo?"

"I want to tell you everything." Hedda said. "I just need a little more time."

"I can give you more time." Travis said, "I need to get the bakery remodeled and opened back up that's going to keep me busy for a bit. But, when you get back to town, look out. I'll be waiting for you."

"I hope so," Hedda said softly a look of trepidation in her eyes.

Travis squeezed her hand reassuringly and grinned at her. Hedda squeezed her thighs together against the onslaught of dampness that had been building since they'd met. She really needed to do something about this attraction. She just wasn't ready to admit that fate had provided her with her one true love to finally break the curse that she'd lived with for so long.

Bjorn had done a serious number on her head and her heart. She wasn't ready to trust one man with her love.

Smiling, but still worried for the state of her heart Hedda turned her hand over in his and intertwined their fingers together. Squeezing slightly. Travis returned the squeeze and smiled back at her.

CHAPTER 11

Travis watched the uneasy look on Hedda's face as she continued to hold his hand.

"So, when do you leave?" Travis asked

"Tomorrow afternoon," Hedda replied, "I'll be gone for a while. Almost a month like I said earlier. I can't to wait to see what the bakery looks like when I come back."

"It's going to be amazing, if I do say so myself." Travis said, "I'm hoping the contractor calls…"

Travis was interrupted by the ringing of his phone. Pulling it from his back jeans pocket, he looked at the screen, grinned, and said,

"Speak of the devil."

Hedda laughed, watching Travis speak animatedly on the phone was a treat. He spoke with his whole body. Hand gestures and big movements. She wondered if he was that enthusiastic in bed. With a sigh of longing she saw Travis end his call.

"Well, Ryan, the owner of A1 Contracting and Remodel, will be by tomorrow to give me an estimate." Travis said on a sigh, "I can't believe it's happening so fast."

"I think that you'll like Ryan." Hedda said, "He's a great guy and tells it to you straight."

"He seems to," Travis agreed, "Just from this call alone it feels like he's the right choice for the updates and remodeling I want to accomplish."

Hedda watched Travis's face as he spoke again of his dreams for his professional life. She didn't really want to leave tomorrow, but she didn't have a choice. The moon wouldn't be full anymore after tonight and she had to be back in the lake. No one had ever not come back to the lake after their three day jaunt. Hedda didn't want to be the first one to break the rules of the curse. The stories the Mer had been telling for hundreds of years of the first few fifty years living beneath the surface of the lake were scary, horror filled tales. Of strong warriors not returning with the waning of the moon. Their deaths long and drawn out. Painful and with no reason. Hedda wouldn't go through that, even if they were just tales to keep the Mer in the lake.

"Are you ready to go home?" Travis asked, they'd been trailing around town for hours since lunch. Holding hands, talking and laughing together. Getting to know one another. Travis felt an undeniable pull to Hedda. He wanted to get to know her better. He wasn't happy that she had to leave town for business. But he understood that work was important. By the time she returned the bakery would be remodeled and open for business.

Hedda could see a future. A bright future with Travis, if she could let go of her fears that one day she wouldn't be enough for him. She didn't want to return to the lake. But it was inevitable that she would. Next month. Next month she would allow Travis to touch her mark. Then she would answer all of his questions.

Hedda looked up and smiled at Travis. After several seconds she said,

"I'll come and find you when I get back, if that's ok?"

"I wouldn't have it any other way." Travis replied, "Can I get your phone number before you leave town?"

"Well, I'll be really busy." Hedda stalled, trying to think of a reason to not give him her number. She knew it would be awkward if she didn't answer or call him back for almost a month. "I may not be able to answer my phone. You can call and leave me a message though, if you want to."

"That would be fine, I could leave you a message and you can just call me back." Travis said.

"Ok, my number is 8675309. The area code is 709." Hedda rattled off her number as Travis typed it into his cell phone. "But remember, I may not be able to answer and depending on what is going on I might not be able to call you back right away."

"That's ok, as long as we can talk at some point." Travis said.

"I'll try my hardest." Hedda promised.

They stared at each other for several silent minutes. Blinking, Travis reached for Hedda, snaking his hands to the nape of her neck, he gave a gentle tug. Their lips met in a fiery kiss. Hedda hadn't ever felt this depth of emotion in a single kiss. She didn't want it to end, but she knew that until she could trust her heart that she'd have to go back into the lake. On a pleased sigh, she broke the kiss gasping for breath, her eyes glazed over with passion. Travis stared down into Hedda's eyes a grin on his lips. The thoughts running through his head rushing about. His erection straining against the zipper of his jeans. He was going to need another shower.

"I should probably take you home." Travis sighed. "Are you ready?"

"No, but I think you're right." Hedda said with a smile. "I'd love it if you walked me home."

Taking her hand once more, Travis walked Hedda back to her cabin by the lake.

At the door, Hedda asked,

"Would you like to come in?"

Travis grinned and replied,

"I would. Yes."

Opening the door Hedda and Travis entered the cabin. Once the door was closed behind them, Hedda turned to look at Travis and asked,

"Would you like a drink? Or something to eat?"

With a panty melting smile he answered,

"I'd love something to eat."

Walking forward Travis griped Hedda's shoulders. Pulling her into his body, he lowered his head slowly. Hedda stared up into his eyes, seeing the intent in them she smiled and raised up on her tip toes to meet his lips half-way. Their lips met in a slow burning kiss that turned into a searing meshing of lips, tongues and teeth. Running his hands down her arms to twine their fingers together he deepened the kiss. Ravaging her mouth like a starving man who hadn't eaten in days. Gasping in pleasure, Hedda unclasp her fingers from Travis's and ran her hands up his muscled back. For a baker, he really was built. Like a Greek god of Olympus. Travis took one hand and gripped her left leg, lifting it along his hip, walking her towards the open bedroom door. Breaking their kiss he looked down into her sex drunk eyes and asked,

"Are you sure this is what you want?"

"Yes, I really do want this. And you." Hedda replied, tugging him further into her bedroom. She reached up and pulled his mouth back to her own, slowly running her tongue along the seam of his lips she heard him groan. Smiling against his lips, she felt the back of her knees hit the bed, stopping for a moment to make sure she didn't fall, she kissed Travis again. Slipping her tongue back into his mouth, their tongues began to duel for dominance. Travis won, helping her gently to the bed he laid her down and climbed onto the duvet covered mattress with her. His grin widened as he pushed her tee shirt up her stomach to just below her breasts. Moving down her body, he leaned down and trailed kisses from her bra line down to her buttoned jeans. Breathing in her tantalizing scent, he groaned again.

Hedda looked down her body to the top of his head that was bent over her waist. His hands were making their way back up her belly to her breasts. Moaning in pleasure she raised her upper torso into his palm as he cupped her left breast. All she had in her mind was the feeling of his lips and hands caressing her body. Travis's right hand made its way back to the closure of her jeans, unbuttoning them with one hand he then worked the zipper down as he continued to kiss down her stomach, he inhaled again saying,

"I love how aroused you are. I can't wait to touch you. To feel your wetness on my fingers, my tongue and then my cock."

Hedda groaned out again, lifting her hips she tried to get pressure added to her dripping core, she could feel her orgasm rising just from the attention of his hands and lips on her upper body. Hedda knew that she was moments away from an explosion of pleasure that she'd only ever felt from her own hands and fingers.

Travis drew his nose from the waist of her jeans to her core, as he nuzzled her, his hands pushed her jeans to her ankles. Stopping momentarily to divest her of her jeans, he smiled up at her as she raised one leg and then the other, smirking as her jeans went flying across the small room to land in a pile near the closet. Travis worked his way back up her legs, stopping at her knees he glanced up at the center of her smiling at the dampness of her panties. Aligning his body with hers, he pressed into her center eliciting a gasping moan, her hips rotated upwards. Hedda could feel the hard length of him against her clit.

"Baby, I don't have any condoms with me." Travis said, "I wasn't expecting this to happen."

"I don't have any here at home." Hedda sighed, thinking about the date, she looked at him, smiled and then said,

"I'm clean and my birth control is up to date. I have an IUD so we're good."

"Thank Christ." Travis muttered under his breath. Grinning he rolled his hips bumping her clit through her wet panties.

"Travis, yes...please." Hedda gasped out, her pleasure rising as they ground together. "I need you. Please."

"I've got you," Travis replied, taking one side of her panties into his fist and ripping the fabric. Moving to the other side he repeated his actions.

"Travis," Hedda exclaimed in surprise. "You still have your clothes on...I need you."

"You'll get me soon enough." Travis replied playfully as he moved into her space. Rubbing his engorged cock against her soaking pussy.

"Ahhh, Travis. You're gonna make me cum." Hedda moaned, "Please, please..."

Travis grinned into her eyes and said,

"Help me with my pants, love."

Smirking up at him, Hedda trailed her hands from his shoulders where she'd been gripping him tightly as she rubbed herself against his hardness. Getting to the fly of his jeans, she unbuttoned and unzipped them in seconds.

Pushing his jeans and boxers down over his hips she watched as his hard length escaped his confining clothes. Gasping at his size, she grinned and said,

"I can't wait to feel that moving inside me."

"And I can't wait to feel your pussy tightening on my cock babe." Travis stated, pushing his throbbing cock against her hot, wet center he groaned. Feeling her soaking folds against his flesh almost too much. He rotated his hips again, the head of his cock barely entering her before he pulled back. She was so wet that he wouldn't need to prep her for his cock. But he wasn't going to give up the chance to taste her honey on his tongue. He moved slowly down her body again, pausing to lave her navel with his tongue. Trailing kisses downwards, stopping to admire her neatly trimmed mons. He placed an opened mouth kiss at her entrance, lightly brushing her clit with his nose. Licking slowly from her opening upwards he increased the pressure slightly.

"Ohhhhhhhhh…." Hedda moaned, "Yeah, please. More, I need more."

Travis increased the speed of his tongue on her clit, taking his hand and caressing up her thigh, he placed one finger at her entrance and pushed into her painstakingly slow. Moving his finger in and out, he picked up the pace and inserted a second finger into her wetness. Hedda lifted her hips in time with his slow thrusts. Moaning continuously, and writhing in pleasure. Travis, slowed his tongue on her clit, he could feel her inner walls start to tighten on his fingers. Her impending orgasm trying to break free. Hedda's breathing sped up as Travis replaced his fingers with his probing tongue. Extending his tongue as far as it would go, he licked up into her canal. Curling his tongue upwards he bumped her g spot. Hedda's orgasm could no longer be denied. She broke, screaming out her pleasure as

Travis continued to lick her pussy through her rushing orgasm. Slowing, he lifted his head, smiling up at her. The dazed look in her eyes almost making him cum.

"Are you ready for my dick, baby?" Travis asked huskily.

"I've been ready." Hedda exclaimed, "I need you, now!"

Travis thrust forward, plunging into her wetness all the way to his balls. Moving in and out, quicker with each thrust. He looked into her eyes as he tried to stave off his own pleasure.

"I need you to get there again, baby." Travis gasped out. "I'm not gonna last. Your pussy is so tight and wet. I'm at my breaking point."

"I'm almost there…" Hedda moaned sexily. "Oh god, oh god…I need more. Harder, I need you deeper."

Travis thrust harder into her. His balls tightened, with one more thrust he held himself deep within her as her walls rippled with her second orgasm. He was able to finally let go. With each flex of his dick his cum coated her inner walls. With one more final thrust he yelled out incoherently,

"Hedda! Yes, god yes. Your pussy is holding me so tight. It's so good."

Holding himself within her, he gasped for breath. Smiling down into her eyes he collapsed onto her torso burying his face in her neck he kissed her pulse at the juncture of her shoulder and collarbone. Grinning when she began to squirm, he raised himself up on his elbows and looked into her beautiful face saying,

"I could get used to this."

"Me too." Hedda sighed out as Travis rolled them to their sides dragging her leg over his own and holding her tightly. Her head cradled at the crook of his shoulder and neck. Hedda ran her fingers lightly over his chest, as she lay thinking of having to wait for almost a month before seeing him again.

"Can you stay?" Hedda asked. "I'd like to see you before I have to leave tomorrow."

"I'd love that," Was his reply. "I'd love that a lot."

Kissing her forehead, Travis sighed contentedly and squeezed her to his side. He watched as her eyes fell closed, a small smirk on her lips. He didn't know how long he watched her sleep before he was dragged under.

Waking in the darkness, Hedda startled. Forgetting where she was and who she was with. Looking up into Travis's face, she smiled and then contemplated the best way to wake him. Taking only a moment to think, she slowly made her way down his body. Stopping at his half hard cock, she licked from root to tip, pausing when Travis moaned to make sure he slept on. Other than the moan that escaped, Travis didn't move. Hedda took that as a good sign. Licking the crown of his dick, she slowly licked him like a favorite sweet treat. Not able to wait any longer, she engulfed his cock and worked her mouth down towards his balls. His cock hit the back of her throat and she swallowed, getting the tip into her throat she sucked. Travis moaned again, this time she didn't stop. She continued suckling his cock, working him up into a frenzy as he slept.

"Babe, wha..." Travis startled and moaned as he watched Hedda swallow his cock in the faint moon glow coming from the window by the bed. On a gasp, he came with no warning. His body shuddered with each flex of his cock. He shouted out as he pulled her from his dick and up his body.

"Hedda!"

"Mmmm, tasty." Hedda smiled as she licked her lips. "What else can I do for you?"

"You are amazing, babe." Travis said through his gasps for air, "Now you can ride me. I want to feel your walls tightening on my cock as you cum."

Hedda straddled his still hard dick and impaled herself. Her pussy soaked from her sucking his cock.

"How are you still hard?" Hedda asked, "Especially after cumming so hard."

"It's this tight pussy baby." Travis said, ":I can't get enough."

Hedda started to move as Travis took her hips in his hands and helped her ride him. And ride him she did. Her up and down motions were enough to take him to the brink in moments.

"Babe, I need you to get there." Travis muttered. "I;m not gonna last."

"Almost...I'm almost there." She sighed out. Moving up and down again, she watched as Travis took one hand and moved it up to her left breast, kneading it and tweaking her nipple causing her to gasp in pleasure. He then took his other hand and ran it down her stomach towards where they were joined. His thumb strummed her clit, once and then twice on the third swipe he felt her clench on his dick. That was just what he had been waiting for. His dick flexed once then his cum shot out and coated her inner walls and the entrance to her cervix. Hedda could feel each pulse of his release as she rode out her orgasm. Shuddering, she fell limply on his heaving chest. Rubbing her cheek against his damp skin she said,

"That was nice."

"Nice? Nice? That was amazing." Travis replied on an indrawn gasp of breath.

Travis wrapped his arms around Hedda. Hugging her to him saying,

"Are you sure you have to go out of town? I'm going to miss you."

"Yes, unfortunately. I'm sure." Hedda sighed sadly. "I'll be back soon though. Wait for me…"

"I'll wait." Travis sighed.

CHAPTER 12

Travis watched Hedda sleeping as he put his clothes on. He wasn't looking forward to her being gone, but he needed to get his head together. He had come to Aurora Falls to open a bakery not to find a woman. But what a woman she was. Strong, beautiful, and amazing. Hedda turned over in her sleep and reached a hand out across the bed, not finding Travis laying there must have woken her as her eyes fluttered open and she peered up at Travis. Blinking she said,

"What time is it? Are you leaving?"

"It's about noon." Travis said quietly, "I was about to wake you."

Hedda watched Travis closely wondering if this was when he thanked her and then walked away. Travis watched the emotions play out on Hedda's face, the look she was giving him was one of trepidation and resignation. Trying to appease her he said,

"I wouldn't have left without waking you. I need a goodbye kiss."

Sitting on the side of the bed, he put his arms around

her back and lifter her body upwards. His mouth crashed into hers with vegence. Lust and want flowing through his blood and driving him to deepen the kiss. The sheet fell from Hedda's naked body revealing her hard nipples. She was aroused again. Travis was just as aroused, unbuttoning his jeans he pushed them down his legs as he rose from the bed. Pulling the sheet the rest of the way off of Hedda he lay atop her and gently probed her entrance with his cock.

"Don't tease, I need you again." Hedda complained on a mewl. "I want your cock. Now. Please."

"You don't have to beg baby," Travis said as he bottomed out, balls deep. Hedda's wetness coating his dick and her walls rippling along his shaft as he thrust in and out of her. In, her pussy would flutter. Out, her cunt tightened not wanting to lose his large hard cock from her grasping pussy. Hedda moaned out salaciously, crying out Travis's name as she came.

"Travissss!"

"Oh yeah, baby that's it cum. Cum for me.' Travis gritted his teeth as he tried to think of anything other than how amazing her clenching pussy felt on his shaft. Unable to derail his orgasm, he shot his cum deep within her body for a third time.

Shuddering, Travis withdrew his deflating dick and kissed Hedda fiercely.

"I have to go baby," Travis said. "I don't want to but you need to get ready to go out of town on business."

"I know. I really enjoyed our time together." Hedda agreed. "I'll be counting down the days until we can see each other again."

"Me too, baby." Travis said, "Me too."

Travis rose and redressed. With a kiss and smile he left Hedda's cabin and headed back to the resort to shower and change.

Hedda laid in bed for a few more minutes after Travis left before rising and heading into the shower. She wasn't ready to give herself fully to Travis, heart and soul. Her body she could give. Her heart was another matter entirely.

CHAPTER 13

Hedda finished closing up her cabin for the month, it was almost dark and she still had an errand to run. Gathering her things she headed for Tait and Phe's home just down from her own cabin.

Knocking on the door, she waited for someone to answer. Hearing a baby crying she stood, thinking of a child with brown hair and blue eyes. Shaking her head as the door opened she looked up and said,

"Hi, Phe. How are you?"

"I'm doing well Hedda." Phe answered with a smile. "How are you doing?"

"I'm good," Hedda replied, smiling at the baby in Phe's arms. "Let me have that gorgeous baby."

Phe handed Amanda over without any preamble saying,

"Some on in. Tait's in the kitchen."

Hedda followed Phe down the hall grinning at the young baby she held in her arms. Entering the kitchen, she stopped and looked at Tait. He was standing at the center island, wearing a pink apron and coating steaks in some sort of sauce. Hedda laughed aloud and said,

"I never thought I'd see the day that you'd be in the kitchen, wearing an apron no less. Wait, are you barefoot? Pregnant?"

"Really funny, Hedda." Tait replied with a grin, not taking any offense to his clanswoman's joke at his expense.

Handing off baby Amanda to Tait after he'd put down the basting brush he was holding. Hedda laughed and grabbed the gift wrapped necklace she'd made for Phe from her pocket. Handing the present off, she watched as Phe smiled and said,

"What's this? You didn't have to get me anything."

"I know. I wanted to though." Hedda said, "You've become a really good friend to me and I wanted to show you how much that means."

Phe stared at the gift for several moments before opening the small package. Once the wrapping was removed she stared at the amazing work that hung from a long leather cord.

"Oh my gosh," Phe exclaimed, "Where in the world did you find this? I love it."

"I made it," Hedda replied.

"What?" Phe said, "You make jewelry? This is amazing. You could make some really good money doing this."

"I do it for fun and relaxation." Hedda said, "Not profit. I have more than enough money."

Phe was flabbergasted. She'd never seen a more beautiful piece of work. Taking the necklace, she slipped it over her head, the stone lay just above her breasts. Tait's eyes heated as he watched Phe adjust the cord and stone to sit flat on her exposed skin.

"Ok, that's my cue to leave." Hedda said on a laugh. "I'm headed back to the lake. I'll see you in a few weeks."

Hedda left the house, laughing as she heard Tait rumbled words of encouragement. She then heard the baby give an excited squeal. Shaking her head, she went down to the lakeshore, joining the others as they began to remove their clothes. Naked she waded into the waters of Sapphire Lake, off to her left she saw the Sapphire Lake Serpent break the surface and begin to swim closer to the shore. Ever watchful. Always protective.

As she hit waist deep in the water, her legs became a long tail of green and gold and blue. The hue a mixture of deep and bright colors. Once her tail was fully formed, she dove under and headed for her cave, to spend a month thinking of and pining for Travis.

Hedda spent her month alone under the waters of Sapphire Lake mining for moonstone and thinking of the night she'd spent with Travis. She couldn't wait to get back to the surface so she could tell him everything she wanted to say. Hedda was impatient to share her history with him. They were Fated and meant to be and she was ready to go all in, heart and soul.

CHAPTER 14

Travis spent his month from Hedda thinking of her and working with the Ryan to get the bakery up and running. The remodel was a success and it was almost time to open the bakery.

Travis was becoming a little discourage though. He'd called and left Hedda several messages over the last three weeks and he'd yet to hear back from her. At this point, he was feeling like he'd been given the slip.

Travis had moved into the small cabin that had come with the purchase of the bakery. The remodeling and rebranding were finally done and Sweet DeTails was set to open in just a few days. On the morning after the full moon the doors would open and he'd welcome his customers. The remodel had taken a little longer than expected, but the delays were well worth it.

He's spent his days on the remodeling and consulting with Ryan and his nights hanging out at The Saucy Wench enjoying a nightly brew and speaking with Orion and the other patrons. One patron, Tom was a riot. Always telling tales of mermaids and lake monsters. Poor guy was a little off his rocker and always holding up the same barstool at the end of the long bar. Enjoying a few too many Mermaid's Breath brews to be sober, at all. But he was harmless and pretty funny.

Travis was just leaving the bar when he looked across the street to the lake to see Hedda. She was standing on the shore line, staring at The Saucy Wench, indecision on her face. When she saw Travis, she smiled and waved. Waiting a split second before breaking into a quick jog. Travis was almost not prepared for the onslaught when she jumped into his arms and kissed him like a starving woman.

"I (*kiss*) missed (*kiss*) you (*kiss*) so (*kiss*) much." Hedda exclaimed.

Travis was in shock, he thought for sure that Hedda had decided he was more of a one night stand than relationship material after not returning any of his calls and messages. Looking at her as she continued to kiss him, he finally broke free from his paralysis and kissed her back. It was like coming home. This kiss, was the beginning of everything.

"I missed you too." Travis said, once Hedda stopped kissing him and looked into his eyes. "You didn't return my calls, I thought maybe we were done before we ever really began."

"There's a reason I couldn't return your calls." Hedda said, "Can we go somewhere private to talk?"

"Sure, of course." Travis replied, "We can go to my place, if that's alright?"

"That's perfect, actually." Hedda said, "I have so much to talk with you about."

CHAPTER 15

Travis took Hedda's hand and they walked together towards the bakery. Hedda stopped walking when they reached the front of the bakery. Gazing in awe at the display in the window. Her free hand went to her mouth to silence the gasp that tried to escape. Travis watched Hedda's face, wondering why she looked like she would cry. He looked at the window, expecting to see something amiss. Instead, he saw the four tier cake display that he'd put in the window earlier in the day. It was riot of greens, blues and golds. A water serpent curled around all four layers. It's head ending just above the top tier. It's golden eyes staring down on the mermaid that rested on the top of the cake, gold leaf accenting the scales on her beautiful tail. The mermaid had Hedda's hair and eyes, as he'd not been able to stop thinking of her. Even when she didn't return his calls.

"How? How did you know?" Hedda asked quietly.

"How did I know what?" Travis returned.

"What I look like in the water?" Hedda said.

"Um, what?" Travis asked, thinking that Hedda maybe

wasn't playing with a full deck of cards. "I was told a tall tale of mermaids and water serpents at the bar. It inspired this cake and I couldn't stop thinking of you when I was molding the mermaid."

Hedda looked up into Travis's eyes and saw the doubt there. She wanted to tell him everything about herself. But she knew it would be easier if he'd just take her hand and place his skin to her mark that rested just above her wrist. She hoped he'd listen to her explanations.

"Can we go somewhere and talk?" Hedda asked, "Please?"

"Yeah, we can." Travis said, "Come on."

Travis took Hedda's hand and they started to walk again. Coming to his small home just past the bakery, he unlocked and opened his door. Going inside, he let Hedda's hand fall to her side and moved to sit on the couch that was against one wall. Patting the cushion next to him he gestured for Hedda to sit down.

Taking a seat, she looked at Travis and said,

"I need you to do me a favor and keep an open mind."

"I'll try, that's all I can promise." Travis said. "What did you want to tell me?"

"It's more what I want to show you." Hedda said, reaching for Travis's hand she opened his fingers and placed his palm on her mark.

Travis jerked as images assaulted his mind. Images of a beautiful yet fierce looking woman standing with her arms upraised to the sky as lightening struck all around her. Words that he shouldn't understand, clear as if it was spoken in English. Images of Viking warriors changing from men and women to water dwelling mermaids and mermen. Time stood still as Travis gasped in outrage. The time Hedda had spent between worlds hurt his heart. He watched as the ship she'd been on sank to the bottom of

Sapphire Lake, the serpent on the prow of the ship changing from wood to flesh. Circling the people as they changed. Flashes of light surrounding them and then nothing. Silence. A watery prison. He could hear other voices trying to counteract the curse that Tamsin had cast.

Travis removed his hand from her wrist. Took in a deep breath and then said,

"What does this mean? Why did you show me all of that?"

"You know why." Hedda whispered, "You saw and heard everything. I would only allow my Fated to touch my mark. And only my Fated can even see the mark."

Travis tried to process all of the images, sounds and information that had hurtled into his mind over the last few minutes. He took Hedda's hand and twined their fingers together. Pulling their hands to his mouth, he turned them to where he could place his lips to her knuckles. After several more minutes, he put their intertwined hands on his leg, which had been nervously bouncing ever since they sat down together.

"Travis," Hedda started to say.

"Hedda, I need to tell you something." Travis said, "I need you to know what I thought while you were gone. I thought you'd been ignoring me when I called and left you messages."

HEDDA STARTED TO WORRY. Had he found someone else? Given up on her when she wasn't able to communicate with him? She hoped not, but she would be understanding. It was a lot to take in. Mer people, serpents and witches. Long lived Vikings. It was almost too much to take.

"I, I get it. I was gone too long." Hedda said quietly, her heart pounding painfully in her chest. "I wish there was a way I could go back and tell you everything when we spent the night in my cabin."

"No, that's not what I'm saying at all," Travis said reassuringly. "What I am trying to say is that yes, I was upset that you hadn't called me back, but now I understand why. I don't want to be without you. I only want you."

Hedda tried to wrap her head around his confession. She had been so sure he'd turn her away that now she was confused, but so happy. Reaching for him, she moved closer to him on the couch. Taking his cheeks between her hands she pulled his head towards her and then she kissed him. Deeply, wetly and thoroughly. She put all of her hope and love into the kiss. Releasing his face, she snaked her arms around his waist and kept kissing him.

CHAPTER 16

Travis pulled away from her and looked into her love filled eyes. Rising from the couch, he took her delicate hand into his own and lead her to his bedroom. Opening the door he walked to his bed and then turned to Hedda. Taking her gently in his arms, he kissed her reverently. Wanting to make the moment last.

As the kiss deepened, their hands seemed to have a mind of their own when they each started to pull the others clothes off. One shirt flying to the left, one shirt flying off to the right. Pants pushed over hips and down legs. Travis released one side of Hedda to run his hand down to her hip, when he touched her hip he found that she was sans panties. Moving them back to the bed he laid her down and then stared at her nakedness. Hunger for her intoxicated him as he covered her body with his own. Slowly kissing down her cheek to her neck, over her collarbone to her shoulder and back again. Trailing open mouthed kisses down to her bare breasts and then to her exposed flat stomach. Not stopping until he reached the apex of her thighs he kissed her mons gently, savoring the closeness of their bodies. As he licked between her folds he could feel her arousal and the intoxicating scent of her drove him a little mad. Licking from her opening to her clit he flicked her small bundle of nerves and watched as she quivered under his attentions. Each swipe of his tongue causing shivers to race across her skin.

"Travis, please…" Hedda begged, panting.

"Please what?" Travis asked teasingly.

"Make me cum." Hedda answered on a moan. "Don't make me wait. I need you."

Travis drove his tongue into her opening. Licking up her honey, thrusting his tongue into her once more he waited a few seconds and replaced his probing tongue with two of his thick digits. Flicking her clit quickly while thrusting his gingers into her rapidly. On a moaning scream Hedda came. A torrent of her release gushing into his awaiting mouth. He lapped at her, prolonging her orgasm until she moaned in semi pain from the over-whelming sensations of his tongue and fingers working her over. Removing his fingers from her body he placed one more open mouthed kiss on her pussy and worked his way back up her body.

Aligning his dick with her center, he pushed into her slowly. Savoring the feeling of her spasming cunt. Bottoming out he started to move slowly at first. Then picking up speed as he continued to hammer into her. Closer and closer to releasing, he rammed his hard dick into her rippling flesh. As she pleasure exploded a second time, he slowed his thrusts. His balls tightened, a shiver raced up his spine. He welcomed his release, he could see colors. Green, blue and gold seemed to spark around them. Their souls aligned and they were joined together.

Hedda took Travis's hand in her own and turned it over to look at his wrist.

"Look love," Hedda said with tears on her cheeks, "We're one now, forever. My curse is broken."

"Does that mean you won't have to return to the lake again?" Travis asked, still dazed from the amazing orgasm that had joined them together.

"I'm here, on land for as long as I live." Hedda said. "I can't wait to spend the rest of my life with you."

Kissing Hedda on the cheek, Travis rolled them to their sides and held her against his body. Marveling at this amazing woman who now belonged to him as he belonged to her. Forever.

EPILOGUE

Travis and Hedda spent the rest of the night talking, laughing and making love. When it was time to go into the bakery he was tired. But it was absolutely worth every sleepless minute they'd spent together. Every touch, every kiss, every word was written on his memory like pictures in a scrapbook.

Arriving at the bakery, Travis unlocked the door and stepped inside. Breathing in the wonderful smells from the previous day, he smiled. He still couldn't believe he'd gotten his dream. The bakery and Hedda, his woman.

Starting the days baking, he puttered around the kitchen. Mixing dough for bread. Adding chocolate chips to the cookie dough and cake mixes. Humming as he worked he didn't hear when Hedda entered the back door. Silently walking up behind Travis who was bent over adding flour to the Hobart mixer, she grabbed his sides and yelled,

"Boo!"

"Dang it!" Travis exclaimed as he jumped, hitting his

head on the top of the floor mixer. Laughing at her antics, he turned and wrapped Hedda in his arms.

"What are you doing here?" Travis asked between kisses. "I left you sleeping in our bed."

" I missed you." She replied simply. "Plus I wanted to help out in the bakery today. To see what it is you do."

"I won't turn down free help." Travis said.

"Who said my help was free?" Hedda said with a wink and a smile.

Travis laughed aloud again. When the bell on the front door jingled, he squeezed her hand and greeted the couple who were standing at the full display case,

"Welcome to Sweet DeTails. What can I get you?"

The man standing at the counter turned to the obviously pregnant woman at his side and asked,

"Sami, what did you want for breakfast, beautiful?"

"I'd love something filled with chocolate." Sami answered, "Marcus, look they have chocolate filled croissants."

Marcus smiled down into Sami's eyes and placed one hand on her distended belly. Rubbing in gentle circles he said,

"I guess our boy wants chocolate."

"Marcus!" Sami exclaimed, "You weren't supposed to tell me until we went home to Washington!"

"I couldn't wait, love." Marcus grinned roguishly, "I wanted to tell you while we were on our babymoon, as you keep calling it."

Travis and Hedda watched as the couple gently kissed, obviously deep in love and happy. On a sigh Hedda said,

"I can't wait until we start our family."

"How soon are you wanting to start?" Travis asked a little worried, "I'd like to spend some time alone with you first."

Marcus and Sami laughed at the expression on Travis's face. Shaking her head Hedda said,

"Obviously not right now. But I don't want to wait to long either. I'm not getting any younger you know."

"This is true." Travis agreed, Hedda scoffed and smacked his arm.

"Let me get you that croissant." Hedda said on a laugh, opening the case and placing the sweet treat on a plate.

"Thank you." Sami said, "Do you have decaf? I'm not allowed full octane until after this one is born."

"We do, let me get that for you." Travis answered, "What about for you? Would you like coffee sir?"

"That would be great thanks." Marcus answered laughing. "I'd like full octane though."

Sami mock glared at her husband and then laughed.

"You're just so funny..."

"You know I'm only playing," Marcus replied, "I'll drink the decaf with you too."

Sami and Hedda shared a look of understanding. A look that said my man is amazing, wonderful and supportive. A look that said, I've finally found the man of my dreams.

"That will be eight dollars and fifty cents." Travis said after pouring two cups of decaf for the expectant couple.

"Here you go, I'm Marcus and this is my wife, Sami." Marcus introduced himself to Travis.

"This is Hedda, my girlfriend and I'm Travis. I own the bakery." Travis replied, "I hope you enjoy your breakfast and your stay in our little town."

"So far it's been a dream." Sami said on a happy sigh, "We're here on vacation before the baby comes. We just found out not that long ago..and this one was supposed to keep the babies gender secret until we got home so we could share it with everyone in Fall City."

"I couldn't wait babe." Marcus said, "Besides, you know that Regan and the boys will know that I couldn't keep it to myself. I can't keep a secret to save my life."

The group laughed at that statement as Sami agreed with Marcus. After their breakfast was gone, they thanked Hedda and Travis and headed back to the resort. They said for a nap, but the look in their eyes gave them away. Nap was definitely a euphemism for wild monkey sex.

The day passed quickly, when it was time to close the bakery they did it together. Laughing and teasing one another as they completed the end of day tasks. Travis and Hedda headed home to his cabin and spent the rest of the night loving each other. In too many ways to count.

THE END

UNTITLED

Thank you for reading Sweet DeTails: Mountain Mermaids: Sapphire Lake, I hope you enjoyed this continuing journey into an all new world.

If you enjoyed the book, please think about leaving a review. Reviews help authors, a lot.

OTHER TITLES BY PA VACHON

Bears in Love series

Mated to the Grizzly

When I See Her Smile

Bearly Mistaken

Marcus: Prequel to the Bears in Love

Olympic Wolves series

Lone Wolf's Woman

Sassy's Desired Mate releasing 2019

Coming soon:

Olympic Wolves series

Wolf's Fated Mate release date TBD

Lake Alice Shifters series

A Brother's Treasure releasing 2019

A Brother's Fate release date TBD

Connect with me online:

www.facebook.com/pa.vachonauthor.33

You can find more information on my books at my website and sign up for my monthly

newsletter here:

www.sexyshifterromance.com

Follow me on Bookbub for all new release updates

www.bookbub.com/profile/pa-vachon

Keep Reading for a sneak peek at Lone Wolf's Woman

Prologue

Memphis stood staring from her second story window watching the rain fall. New Orleans in June was always wet. Considering it stayed in the mid-seventies to the high eighties the rain was a humid, hot, and oppressive experience. Having lived here since her parents died when she was eight, she was used to the weather. What she wasn't used to was the way her uncle had started locking her in her room when she was home from her shopping and visiting excursions. She hadn't left the house in two weeks. Things needed to change.

It started in late April and so far, she'd been stuck in her room reading and staying out of her uncle's way. The last time Memphis had asked him why he was holding her prisoner, Uncle Charles had sneered and said in a deadly voice,

"You'll see soon enough."

Memphis stopped asking after that reaction. Afraid of what he'd do to her if she voiced her questions again.

Last night after dinner, her uncle hadn't stayed long enough to lock her in. He'd directed one of the maids to do it. The maid took pity on her when her uncle went into his office to take a phone call. Memphis was able to sit in the kitchen and visit with the staff. After talking for a while Memphis excused herself to go to the restroom. Walking by her uncle's office she could hear his raised voice, yelling at some unknown person on the phone. Memphis stopped, tiptoed to the office door and quietly pressed her ear to the door. She knew this was the only way that she'd find out what was happening.

"What do you mean you won't pay more than Five Hundred Thousand?" Charles yelled into the phone. "You agreed on a million dollars to take my niece off my hands."

Memphis gasped. Now she knew why Uncle Charles had kept her locked behind closed doors. He was trying to sell her. Trying to calm her racing heart she listened closer.

"I have other offers," he yelled, "I can get top dollar for Memphis. She's a virgin and an heiress. I gave you first right of refusal because we've been business associates for so long."

Memphis made her way from the office door. Her mind racing, heading up the stairs she started to plan her escape.

Meanwhile, 2700 miles away...

Atticus "Gus" Redtree was confused, again. He'd just been dumped. Again. By someone who he'd thought he could build a life with. He'd given up hope of finding a mate, that was a fairy tale, at least for him. He'd always been the 'rescue the damsel' type, he was drawn to women who seemed to need a hand up. Like Lorraine, she'd been the first but not the last. He'd come upon her at the Wolf's Den, the local watering hole run by one of his best friends and pack mates, Sassy Lynn Smith. Lorraine had had a few too many and was being dragged unwilling, kicking and fighting from the bar by a large, unkempt man that Gus had never seen before. He got up from his normal bar stool and headed towards the door.

"Hey man, what's going on?" Gus asked.

"Mind your business, prick." The man had slurred.

"Well, usually I would friend," Gus said, "But, it doesn't

look like the lady wants to go with you."

"Fuck off!" The man slurred loudly, "You need to get the hell outta my face."

"I can't do that." Gus said, "But thanks for the advice."

Reaching forward Gus had removed the drunkard's hand from around the lady's wrist. Shocked the guy had taken a swing. It bounced off of Gus's abs like a fly, irritating but ineffective. With a grin, Gus slugged the man, watching him hit the floor with a thud he turned to the obviously drunk woman and said,

"Are you ok, darlin'"

"I'm, I'm fine," she said, "Thank you, I didn't want to go with Daryl. He's been getting more and more pushy lately."

"No problem, do you need a ride," Gus asked, "I can take you to your house or if you don't live around here to the hotel in town."

The woman took a moment to think, then said,

"I'm Lorraine, I would love a ride."

From there, they were inseparable. For about three months, then he came home from work one afternoon and Lorraine said,

"I'm done with this."

"Done with what, hun?" Gus asked bewildered.

"This thing we're doing." Lorraine said pointing between them, "I appreciate all you've done for me, but my life isn't here. I need excitement. I need the city. I have to go. Thanks, for everything."

Gus watched as she left. He still couldn't believe she'd gone. He watched the same way when Amy, Renee and Stef had done the same thing. He'd heard later down the line that each had left town, settled in the Seattle area and had long term relationships with other men. Lorraine had even married since that day five years before. He really needed to stop helping damsels. Especially the pretty ones.

CHAPTER ONE

Memphis was out of time and out of options. She knew her uncle would eventually figure out that she'd headed to the Olympic Peninsula, to just outside of Lake Quinault where her cabin was located. It was left to Memphis by her maternal grandmother in her last will and testament. What she hadn't expected was for her new to her car to break down in the middle of a freak summer thunderstorm. The rain started just outside Olympia, and it was vastly different than any Louisiana rain storm. Memphis had gotten off the I5 freeway to head west towards the coast road highway. At first it was no big deal, just some rain. As she got closer to the Olympic National Forest it had turned into a deluge, hard driving rain that was falling sideways...and then the thunder and lightning had started. She thought she'd beat the storm, ten miles from her destination and her car sputtered and then died an agonizingly loud death. Looking down at her cell, she discovered that she had no bars and very little charge. She really needed to get to a phone store to replace her charger, it just wasn't working right.

Memphis debated whether to get out of the car and check under the hood. Memphis was definitely no mechanic, she'd been a pampered princess kept under lock and key after her parents had died in a car accident when she was eight years old. Her father's brother, her uncle Charles, had said it was to keep her safe. When really, he'd only wanted to keep her from other people. Once she hit eighteen her uncle had started to act differently. Always asking her what she wanted to do with her life. She'd answered that particular question the same way every time. She wanted to be an artist, a painter just like her mother before her. Memphis wanted to paint majestic landscapes and life like portraits. That was one of the reasons she'd escaped from her locked room and ran for the rainforest of Washington state. That and the fact that her uncle had sold her to the highest bidder, like a Thoroughbred racehorse that bred the high stakes winners for the Kentucky Derby.

Right now, wasn't the time to think about her Uncle Charles and the man she'd been auctioned off to. Kyle Davies was in her rear-view mirror and that's where he and her uncle would both stay. She needed to get back on the road. Letting her head fall to the steering wheel in defeat, she took a deep breath, pulled the engine release and opened the driver's door of her car. Huddled against the driving rain, she made her way to the front of the car and opened the hood, using her phone as a flashlight she stared into the dark abyss that was the engine compartment of her small sedan. Looking, but not knowing what anything was. She sighed loudly, the sound lost in the torrent of the rain. Slamming the hood closed, she rushed back to the driver's side of her car. Soaked from head to toe, she sat shivering in the seat. It may have been mid-summer, but even mid-summer could be chilly on the peninsula.

After slamming her door closed, Memphis let her head fall back on the headrest of her seat. Closing her eyes, she did something she'd not done in years, she asked for assistance from the one being she'd stopped believing in when she was just eight years old. She asked God to get her out of this predicament. Little did she know, she'd get her answer in the form of a large hunk of a gorgeous man.

Memphis had been sitting with her head back and her eyes closed for so long she'd almost fallen asleep. Hearing a loud bang, she startled, looking to her left she saw the shadow of a very large man knocking on her driver's window. When he saw that she'd looked his was, he pantomimed rolling the window down. Not sure what to do, Memphis lowered the window an inch and then leaned over to hear the man speak.

"Hey, are you ok?" The man asked, "Do you need help?"

"Um, hi." Memphis replied, "Yes. No. Well, maybe. I'm not sure what happened. It died."

"Can you tell me what the car did before it died?" He asked, "Did it make any noises or anything?"

"Well, not really." Memphis said, "It kind of sputtered, then died."

"I'm not a mechanic," the man stated, "But, I know a little about cars. Pop your hood and I'll take a look for you. Where were you headed?"

"That would be great, thanks." Memphis answered as she pulled the hood latch for the second time, "I was headed for Lake Quinault. I have a cabin near there."

"Nice, I live just outside of town myself," He said, "By the way, my name is Atticus. Atticus Redtree, but you can call me Gus. Everyone does."

"Hi, Gus. It's nice to meet you." Memphis replied, "My name is Memphis. Memphis Rose."

Gus headed for the front of the car and opened the

hood. Memphis debated whether or not to go back out into the rain. Deciding she was soaked already, and it wouldn't matter she left her car and walked to where Gus was standing fiddling with one of the lines (or were those hoses) of her old beater.

"So, it looks like the battery cables are bad." Gus said pointing to where the cables were connected on the top of the battery, "There's a lot of corrosion here on the terminals. I can take you into town to the repair shop and then have your car towed to the shop that's in town."

"That would be great," Memphis said enthusiastically, she was ready to get warm and dry. "Let me just grab my overnight bag from the car."

Gus watched as Memphis walked to the back of the car, lifting the trunk lid she leaned in, he could just see the outline of her in the darkening twilight. It was an image that would be burned into his brain for quite some time. Gus headed for his own vehicle to clean out the passenger side floorboard. He was not the best at keeping his rig clean, at least on the inside. Memphis slammed the trunk and made a quick beeline for lifted 4x4 that was parked in front of her car. She paused before getting into the opened door.

"I mean I appreciate the ride and all," Memphis said worriedly, "But, should I be worried? You might be a serial killer for all I know."

"I might be," Gus agreed with a smile and a laugh, "but the only cereal killing I've done is to the bowl of Cocoa puffs I ate for breakfast earlier today."

Memphis gave a relieved laugh and climbed up into the truck, no small feat as she was only 5'3" and had to use the sidestep and the oh shit handle.

"Thank you, Gus for doing this," Memphis said, "I wasn't sure how I was going to get into town."

"It's not a problem at all," Gus answered, turning to look at Memphis with a grin. "Do you want to go to the motel after the auto repair shop? Or, I can take you to your cabin if you'd like?"

Memphis thought about it for several minutes, not sure if she could trust this man. He was nice to stop, but did he want to get her alone at the cabin to do nefarious things to her?

"Um, I 'll let you know once I'm done with the auto repair shop," Memphis said with a smile, "Then I'll know where to go from there."

"Sounds good, doll." Gus answered on a husky laugh, starting his truck and pulling away from the side of the road. "You want to listen to some music?"

"Sure, whatever you'd like to listen to," Memphis said, "Well, anything but no jazz music, it puts me right to sleep."

Gus laughed out loud then leaned over to turn on the radio, tuning in a country station. Blake Shelton was singing about a honey bee. Such weird music, but cute.

CHAPTER TWO

Pulling up to Ray's Auto Repair, Gus put his truck into park and shut off the engine. Memphis had sat quietly in the passenger seat, deep in thought she hadn't noticed that the truck had stopped until Gus opened his door. Walking around the front of the truck, he reached for her door handle and opened her door. Memphis slid from the seat with a smile aimed at Gus.

"Thank you." Memphis said, "I hadn't noticed we'd arrived."

"No problem," Gus answered, "My momma would skin me alive if I didn't treat you right. Like a lady."

Memphis grinned, with a laugh she said,

"Well we wouldn't want your momma to give you what for now would we."

Memphis and Gus made their way to the front door of the repair shop. Pushing the door open, Gus called out,

"Ray, hey Ray, where you at man? I have a customer here. Her car needs a tow back into town, the battery cables and terminals are corroded and could probably stand with a cleaning, if not a new battery all together."

From the back of the shop a loud bang could be heard, followed by "Shit" said in a gravelly tone. Then footsteps could be heard, along with some interesting muttering.

"Dang it, Gus." Ray said loudly, "What have I told you about yelling through the shop like that?"

"Oops, sorry man," Gus replied, "Are you ok?"

"Yeah, I'm fine. No thanks to you and your yelling." Ray said. "So what kind of car and where is it at?"

It's an older Toyota Camry. It belongs to Memphis. Memphis this is Ray, Ray this is Memphis." Gus said, "It's on the side of the road about twenty minutes south on the coast highway."

"Sure, sure I'll pick it up and get the work done," Ray said, "Nice to meet you Memphis. The repairs will cost labor for sure, but if the cables need changed out or the battery needs to be replaced it will be a little more. Labor is seventy-five an hour. The job will probably take me thirty minutes or so."

"Uhhh, that should be fine," Memphis said, "I'm not sure how soon I'll be able to pay for the repairs. I guess I'll need to get a job."

"We'll figure it out," Gus assured her, "Don't worry about it just yet. Give Ray your keys and I'll get you to your place or the local hotel for you to get settled in."

Memphis handed Ray her keys. Gus motioned for her to follow him as they headed out the front door, she made the decision to have Gus take her to her cabin. She was ready to see where her mom's family was from.

"Gus, can you take me to the cabin?" Memphis asked, "I'd really like to get settled as soon as possible."

"Sure, it's no problem," Gus answered, heading to the passenger side of his truck and opening her door for her. With a lifted eyebrow and grin she got into the truck and then watched as Gus walked around to his door and got in.

Closing his door, he started up his truck, and looked at Memphis.

"So, I'm going to need some directions…" Gus said, "Where's your cabin at?"

"It's located at 215 Sweet Briar Drive," Memphis said, "Do you know where that is?

"As a matter of fact, I do." Gus replied with a smile, "I live on the same street, three cabins down. What a small world huh?"

"I guess it is," Memphis said with a hearty laugh. "I'll know where to go if I need any sugar."

Gus drove straight to Sweet Briar Drive. Pulling up to the house at 215, he let out a surprised whistle and said,

"I think this place has seen better days. It's gonna need a lot of work before you can live here."

Memphis stared forlornly out the windshield, wondering why the cabin was so rundown, the will provided for a caretaker. It looked like no one had been to the cabin since her grandmother had passed away two years before.

"So, I see," Memphis said with a defeated sigh, "I hate to ask but can you take me to the hotel. I'm really gonna need a job now. I won't have enough money for any of the repairs for a while."

"Hey, don't worry. I can take you to the hotel, but do you have funds for the stay? I'd hate for you to be stuck." Gus said, trying to make Memphis smile again, "It will be fine. I know someone who's hiring. My friend Sassy at the Wolf's Den. She's always looking for more waitresses. We can stop there on the way to the hotel."

Memphis looked out the window for several more minutes, biting her lip. Deep in thought she didn't see Gus watching her. His eyes glued to her face.

"Um, I have a little money saved up," Memphis sighed,

"But, I don't know how long it will last me. I could definitely use a job. I would appreciate an introduction to Sassy."

"Well, first things first. Let's go to the hotel and get you checked in," Gus said, "Then we can stop at the Wolf's Den for dinner and an introduction."

Gus started his truck and put it in reverse, leaving the driveway he took a quick look at Memphis and asked,

"Do you mind if we stop by my place for a minute? I need to grab a different shirt if that's ok with you?"

"That's fine, I don't want to inconvenience you." Memphis replied, "I can wait in the truck while you change."

"You don't have to stay in the truck." Gus said, turning on his blinker he pulled up to a cabin that resembled Memphis's the only difference was that Gus's cabin wasn't falling apart at the seams. "You should come in and take a look around, my cabin used to look a lot like yours before I renovated it."

"Sounds good." Memphis replied, "Thank you for all of your help today."

Gus opened his door after turning off his truck/car. Walking around the hood, he stopped to open the passenger door for Memphis, with a slight blush she slid from the seat and said,

"Always the gentleman. Thank you, Gus."

"Come on trouble," Gus said on a laugh, while grabbing her hand and leading her to the front door, "Let's go inside."

Gus moved to the side when they reached his front porch, letting Memphis go ahead of him. He followed her up the steps. He never could resist a damsel in distress. He just hoped this time he didn't

. . .

GET HIS HEART STOMPED ON. Opening the front door, he motioned for Memphis to enter his cabin. Once inside he closed the door.

"Head on into the kitchen, grab something to drink if you want." Gus said, "I'm going to go change real quick then we can go."

"Sounds good, where are your glasses? I'd love a glass of water." Memphis said.

"They're in the cupboard to the left of the sink," Gus answered as he headed down the short hallway, "Help yourself, there's water in the fridge or you can drink tap. I'm on a natural spring here so the water tastes amazing."

Memphis watched as Gus headed down to his room, the way he walked was full of raw power. His gait more of a stalk than an actual walk. Shaking her head, she turned towards the kitchen and went to the sink. Opening the cupboard, she pulled a glass from the shelf. Turning on the cold tap she let it run for a few seconds to let it get cold. Filling the glass, she looked out the window that was over the sink, the backyard of Gus's cabin was mostly woods with a small patch of grass just beyond the covered back patio. Sipping her water, she was lost in thought and didn't hear Gus come into the kitchen.

"Hey, how's the water?" Gus asked.

Jumping a bit, Memphis turned and answered,

"It's good. Nice and cold. No chemicals like back home from the tap."

"Back home?" Gus asked. "Where are you from? I can hear a bit of an accent but can't quite place it."

"Recently of New Orleans. But I'm originally from upstate New York." Memphis stated, "My parents and I lived in Lake Placid until their car accident. Then I moved to Louisiana with my Uncle."

Memphis stopped talking abruptly, not knowing why

she was spewing so much information about her life. She needed to stay under the radar. Her uncle had more than enough money to find her if she let her guard down. She wasn't ready to be Mrs. Kyle Stanton the third. He was twenty years her senior and thrice married. His wives had all gone on by mysterious means.

With a wane smile, Memphis said,

"We should probably go. I need to check into the hotel still."

"You're right," Gus agreed, "We should go. Lead the way beautiful."

Memphis laughed, shaking her head in disbelief she headed for the front door.

Made in the USA
Columbia, SC
26 September 2023